Imprint
A part of Macmillan Publishing Group, LLC
120 Broadway, New York, NY 10271

About This Book
The text was set in Delm SemiLight and the display type is CoconPro.
The book was edited by John Morgan and Nicole Otto and designed by Elynn Cohen.
The production was supervised by Raymond Ernesto Colón, and the production editor was Dawn Ryan.

Library of Congress Cataloging-in-Publication Data is available.

ISBN 978-1-250-19033-8 (hardcover)

Our books may be purchased in bulk for promotional, educational, or business use.
Please contact your local bookseller or the Macmillan Corporate and Premium Sales Department
at (800) 221-7945 ext. 5442 or by email at MacmillanSpecialMarkets@macmillan.com.

Imprint logo designed by Amanda Spielman

First edition, 2019

10 9 8 7 6 5 4 3 2 1

mackids.com

The Rangers are needed to protect the Earth
Just as only you can protect this book's worth,
So you better not take it without paying its cost,
Or before the battle's begun, it's already lost.

Rainbow Rangers

The Quest for the Confetti Crystal

Written by Summer Greene

Illustrated by Joshua Heinsz
and Maxime Lebrun

[Imprint]
MAKE YOUR MARK

NEW YORK

THE RAINBOW RANGERS are ready for their next mission.

"Happy one hundredth mission, Bonnie Blueberry!" cheers Rosie Redd as she hops on her Spectra-Scooter.

"She'll be great," says Anna Banana. "And we're going to help!"

"Ride, Rangers, Ride!" shouts Rosie. The three Rainbow Rangers zoom through the top of the Crystal Command Center to save the day!

"We're going to throw Bonnie the perfect party to celebrate her one hundredth mission!" Kalia tells the others. "We'll even use the Confetti Crystal."

"FLOOF!"
Floof chirps happily.

"Guard the crystal while we prepare the cupcakes in the kitchen," says Kalia.

"We're counting on you, Floof!" says Lavender LaViolette. "The Confetti Crystal is super important, but you'll take great care of it."

Floof usually loves going on missions with the Rangers, but now he has an extra special mission of his own!

He brings the crystal to the Kaleidocove and checks it for scratches. It's perfect!

Floof decides it will be safest nestled on top of the soft cushions. "**FLOOF!**" he says.

Looking around the Kaleidocove, Floof realizes it doesn't look like much of a party scene.

Bonnie deserves the most rainbow-tastic party ever,
and that means LOTS of decorations!

"FLOOF!" he cries. First he covers the ceiling with bubbles.

Then he strings bright streamers from side to side. He stands on tippy-hooves to hang the last streamer and . . .

WHOOPS!
The Confetti Crystal
is rolling away!

Floof fires a bubble at the Confetti Crystal, but that only floats it above his head! Before Floof can pop the bubble, a group of Fluttercups swoop in.

"SHINY!" the Fluttercups cheer.

"Floof!" cries Floof.

"We'd *love* to play, Floof!" say the Fluttercups. But that's not what Floof meant at all.

POP! The Fluttercups free the crystal, but then they toss it around! "Catch it, Floof!" they cry.

The Fluttercups throw the crystal over Floof's head
and bounce away down the hall to the Rainbow Tunnel.
"FLOOF!" The prismacorn races after it . . .

But the end of the Rainbow Hall is filled with Dragonflice! They like to use their special powers to freeze things and play slip 'n' glide.

The crystal is quickly sliding away.

The Bunnysus hears all the commotion and hops in on the fun. "**WHEEE!**" she says.

But the ice is too slippery!
The Confetti Crystal soars
right out the window!

Now the crystal will be lost forever!
"**FLOOOOOOF!**" cries Floof.

Luckily, the Bunnysus can fly!
She grabs Floof and carries him
right out the window.
The others cheer them on.

They race through the sky to catch the crystal! It's just out of reach!

Floof shakes his rainbow mane,
takes a big breath, and stretches . . .
And stretches . . .
And stretches!

It's too far! Floof swings his head to whack the crystal with his special Prismacorn horn.

He knocks it back up to the Kaleidocove!

The party is saved!

"Floof, FLOOF!" says
Floof, thanking his new friends.

Floof rushes back to the Kaleidocove to set the crystal in place and finish decorating. He's just in time!

When Bonnie Blueberry returns from her one hundredth successful mission with Anna and Rosie, the perfect party is waiting for her.

"Great job, Floof," Kalia says.
"**Floof!**" puffs Floof.

"Let the celebration begin," Kalia says.

With a wave from Kalia, the Confetti Crystal creates an incredible rainbow of sparkly joy. "FLOOF!"

THE END